# Under the Moon

## Jazz Standards and Lullabies

Performed by Ella Fitzgerald, Louis Armstrong, Nina Simone...

Selected by Misja Fitzgerald Michel Illustrated by Ilya Green

# Willow Weep for Me

**Singer Billie Holiday Words and music Ann Ronell**

Nicknamed "Lady Day" by her close friend Lester Young, Billie Holiday sang with some of jazz's greatest musicians, including Benny Goodman, Louis Armstrong, Duke Ellington and Count Basie. With her gentle, husky voice, shedeveloped a uniquely personal style of singing that had a substantial impact on both vocal and instrumental jazz. The nostalgic lyrics of "Willow Weep for Me" feel like they were written especially for Billie Holiday.

# Gone With the Wind

**Singer Julie London Words Herb Magidson Music Allie Wrubel**

"Gone With the Wind" is a love song whose lyrics bear no relation to either Margaret Mitchell's novel published in 1936 or the epic film that followed and won several Oscars. Known for her deep sensual voice, Julie London was also a motion picture and television actor. She recorded "Gone With the Wind" on the 1955 album *Julie Is Her Name*. The flip side featured "Cry Me a River"—the legendary song that launched her career.

# It Might As Well Be Spring

Singer Nina Simone Words Oscar Hammerstein II Music Richard Rodgers

The things I used to like, I don't like anymore
I want a lot of other things, I've never had before
It's just like my mamma says, I sit around and mourn
Pretending that I am so wonderful and knowing I'm adored

I'm as restless as a willow in a windstorm
I'm as jumpy as a puppet on a string
I'd say that I had spring fever
But I know it isn't spring

I'm as starry-eyed and gravely discontented
Like a nightingale without a song to sing
Oh, why should I have spring fever
When it isn't even spring?

I keep wishing I were somewhere else
Walking down a strange new street
Hearing words that I have never, never heard
From a man I've yet to meet

I'm as busy as a spider spinning daydreams
I'm as giddy as a baby on a swing
I haven't seen a crocus or a rosebud
Or a robin or a bluebird on the wing
But I feel so gay in a melancholy way
That it might as well be spring

Taken from the 1945 film *State Fair,* the song *"It Might as Well Be Spring"* figured in the repertoire of a long list of great performers headed by Ella Fitzgerald and Sarah Vaughan. The song inspired many musicians, notably pianists like Errol Gardner and, more recently, Brad Mehldau and Jacky Terrasson. Nina Simone was on the road to becoming a classical pianist, but racial segregation stood in her way. Turning to jazz by default, the ardent defender of civil rights known as the "High Priestess of Soul" forged her own inimitable style incorporating elements of blues, soul and classical music.

# Come Rain or Come Shine

**Singer** Sarah Vaughan **Words** Johnny Mercer **Music** Harold Arlen

I'm gonna love you like nobody's loved you
Come rain or come shine
High as a mountain and deep as a river
Come rain or come shine
I guess when you met me
It was just one of those things
But don't ever bet me
Cause I'm gonna be true if you let me

You're gonna love me like nobody's loved me
Come rain or come shine
Happy together, unhappy together
And won't it be fine?
Days may be cloudy or sunny
We're in or we're out of the money
But I'm with you always
I'm with you rain or shine

Known as the "Divine One," Sarah Vaughan began singing in the choirs of the church attended by her parents, where she also learned to play piano and organ. In 1942 at the age of 18, she won an amateur singing contest at the Apollo Theatre in Harlem with Ella Fitzgerald in attendance to congratulate her in person. Blessed with an intense, sensual voice, Sarah Vaughan had an extraordinarily wide range. A genuine talent for improvisation allowed her to use her exceptional voice like a musical instrument. Her repertoire extended from variety-style music to jazz and she performed with all the greats of be-bop, including Dizzie Gillespie, Charlie Parker and Art Blakey.

# Stormy Weather

Singers **The Golden Gate Quartet** Words **Harold Arlen** Music **Ted Kochler**

I don't know why there's no sun up in the sky
Stormy weather
Can't get my poor old self together
Keeps raining all the time, all the time

Life is bare, gloom and misery everywhere
Stormy weather
Can't get my poor old self together
Keeps raining all the time, all the time

Since she went away, the blues came in and met me
And if she stays away, old rocking chair's gonna get me
All I do is pray that the Lord will let me
Walk in the sun once more

Life is bare, gloom and misery everywhere
Stormy weather
Can't get my poor old self together, oh Lord
Keeps raining all the time

I can't go on, everything I had is gone
Stormy weather
Just can't get my poor old self together
Keeps raining all the time

"Stormy Weather" was written for Cab Calloway, but it was Ethel Waters who turned it into a hit in 1933 with Duke Ellington on the stage of the Cotton Club in Harlem. Ten years later, the song was taken up by Lena Horne in a 20th Century Fox musical by the same name. All the film's actors were African-American at a time when black performers, even the best, were almost entirely excluded from musicals. The Golden Gate Quartet still performs today, 84 years after the group was founded. Paul Brembly, the current lead singer, ensures that the group remains true to its values of artistic innovation. For more than half a century, a string of talented musicians have succeeded one another in the ranks of the quartet and served as ambassadors of American black music by touring the world.

# Blue Moon

**Singer Mel Tormé Words Lorenz Hart and Richard Rodgers Music Richard Rodgers**

Blue Moon, you saw me standing alone
Without a dream in my heart
Without a love of my own
Blue Moon, you knew just what I was there for
You heard me saying a prayer for
Someone I really could care for
And then there suddenly appeared before me

The only one my arms could ever hold
I heard somebody whisper, "please adore me"
And when I looked, the moon had turned to gold!
Blue Moon, now I'm no longer alone
Without a dream in my heart
Without a love of my own

Originally intended for Jean Harlow, "Blue Moon" underwent many changes to its lyrics and title before finally reaching a definitive version in 1935. Over the years, this jazz standard has continued to inspire great singers. Ella Fitzgerald, Julie London, Nat King Cole and Stevie Wonder are just some of the artists who have brought their unique style to it. The song has also appeared in many movies, including Martin Scorcese's *New York, New York*, Jim Jarmusch's *Mystery Train* (the Elvis Presley version) and, more recently, the Woody Allen film *Blue Jasmine*. One of the loveliest instrumental versions is a harp rendition in *The Marx Brothers at the Circus*, with Harpo surrounded by several African-American extras as he plucks the strings.

# The Snow Is Falling

**Singer Ray Charles** Words and Music by **Jeremy Leiber** and **Mike Stoller**

Snow is falling
Falling on the cold cold ground
Snow is falling, baby
Falling on the cold cold ground
Gloom and misery
Gloom and misery all around

I used to be so happy, now all I do is cry
Well, I used to be so happy, now all I do is cry
Gonna buy myself a coffin
Well, I'm gonna lay right down and die

Well, people if I die tomorrow
Who's gonna cry for me?
Well, if I die tomorrow
Who's gonna cry for me?
Well, I ain't got nothing
But these blues and misery

I guess you better come on and get me
Ain't got nothing to lose
I guess you better come on and get me
Ain't got nothing to lose
Well, I don't feel like living
Life ain't nothing but the blues

Considered a pioneer of soul music, Ray Charles (nicknamed "The Genius" by Frank Sinatra) introduced a new genre, fusing elements of blues with gospel. In 1954, he had his first hit with "I Got a Woman", then went on to conquer white audiences with "Hallelujah I Love Her So". A triumph at Carnegie Hall and tours across Europe soon followed. Ray Charles' career went into decline in the 1970s, but he returned to the forefront in the 1980s and remained popular until his death in 2003. His warm voice and skilful piano playing allowed him to tackle any style: rhythm and blues, jazz, rock and roll, country and more. His best-loved songs include "What'd I Say", "Hit the Road, Jack" and, especially, "Georgia on My Mind", which was later adopted as the state's official anthem.

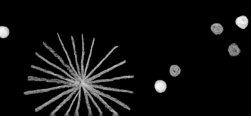

# Winter Wonderland

**Singer** Louis Armstrong **Words** Richard B. Smith **Music** Felix Bernard

Sleigh bells ring, are you listening
In the lane, snow is glistening
A beautiful sight, we're happy tonight
Walking in a winter wonderland

Gone away is the bluebird
Here to stay is a new bird
He sings a love song as we go along
Walking in a winter wonderland

In the meadow we can build a snowman
Then pretend that he is Parson Brown
He'll say, "Are you married?"
We'll say, "No man,
But you can do the job when you're in town"

Later on, we'll conspire
As we dream by the fire
To face unafraid the plans that we've made
Walking in the winter wonderland

Louis Armstrong learned to play the cornet while living at home for delinquent children in New Orleans. He began his career as a member of King Oliver's Creole Jazz Band before going on to form his own ensembles. A virtuoso trumpeter, he became a star in the 1930s on Broadway and in movies. With his distinct raspy voice, he popularized scat—the use of improvised onomatopoeias in place of lyrics. A forerunner of modern jazz, Louis Armstrong had a powerful impact on contemporary musicians with his sense of innovation, vocal and instrumental improvisation techniques.

# Let It Snow! Let It Snow! Let It Snow!

**Singer** Vaughn Monroe **Words** Sammy Cahn **Music** Jule Styne

Oh, the weather outside is frightful
But the fire is so delightful
And since we've no place to go
Let it snow, let it snow, let it snow!

It doesn't show signs of stopping
And I brought some corn for popping
The lights are turned way down low
Let it snow, let it snow, let it snow!

When we finally kiss goodnight
How I'll hate going out in the storm
But if you really hold me tight
All the way home I'll be warm

The fire is slowly dying
And, my dear, we're still good-bye-ing
But as long as you love me so
Let it snow, let it snow, let it snow!

In 1945, Sammy Cahn and Jule Styne were wishing it would snow in Hollywood when they wrote this song during a blistering California heat wave. "Let It Snow" became a big hit for American singer and trumpet player Vaughn Monroe, who also occasionally acted in Westerns and was the frontman for a popular group in the 1940s and 1950s. Although the lyrics never mention Christmas, the song remains a standard on holiday season albums. Countless performers have recorded the song since it was first penned, including Frank Sinatra, Bing Crosby, Ella Fitzgerald and Dean Martin.

# December

Singer **Kay Starr** Words **Al Rinker** Music **Floyd Huddleston**
and **Al Rinker**

December, it always happens in December
I get to yearning for a Christmas I know
With holly and snow
The kind we used to have back home a long time ago

December, brings back a scene that I remember
The lighted Christmas trees and windows at night
So cheerful and bright
And all the world a wonderland all covered with white

Children sound asleep on Christmas Eve
They're dreaming dreams of make-believe
You can bet tomorrow they'll be thrilled
When they awake to find their stockings filled

December, these are the things that I remember
And so no matter what my fortune may be
Or where I may roam
In December, I'll be going home

Born of an Iroquois father and Irish mother, Kay Starr, born Katherine Laverne Starks, began her career on local radio in the 1930s while still a schoolgirl. Following a bout of pneumonia when she was 23, her voice became deeper and more gravelly. Jazz, country, rock, rhythm and blues, gospel—she performed in every style but was especially appreciated by the jazz community. Billie Holiday called her "the only white woman who could sing the blues."

# Winter Weather

Singer **Fats Waller** Words and music **Ted Shapiro**

I love the winter weather
So the two of us can get together
There's nothing sweeter, finer
When it's nice and cold
I can hold my baby
Closer to me

And collect them fine kisses
That are due me
I love the winter weather
Because I've got my love
To keep me warm

Thomas Wright "Fats" Waller, born in 1904, had a stout physique that earned
him the nickname early on. His father, a Baptist minister, taught him the harmonium
and piano. To earn a living, he began playing the organ in movie theatres. His good
sense of humour and penchant for clowning kept audiences in stitches. Although this
comic image endured, encouraged mostly by producers, Fats Waller was also
an excellent musician and a remarkable pianist with a subtle touch.

# What Are You Doing New Year's Eve?

Singer **Ella Fitzgerald** Words and music **Frank Loesser**

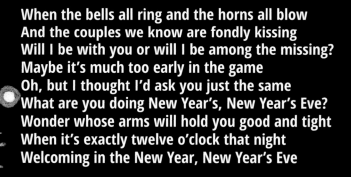

When the bells all ring and the horns all blow
And the couples we know are fondly kissing
Will I be with you or will I be among the missing?
Maybe it's much too early in the game
Oh, but I thought I'd ask you just the same
What are you doing New Year's, New Year's Eve?
Wonder whose arms will hold you good and tight
When it's exactly twelve o'clock that night
Welcoming in the New Year, New Year's Eve

Maybe I'm crazy to suppose
I'd ever be the one you chose
Out of the thousand invitations you receive

Oh, but in case I stand one little chance
Here comes the jackpot question in advance
What are you doing New Year's, New Year's Eve?

Ella Fitzgerald was sixteen when she took to the stage for the first time. Best known as a swing singer, she was also right at home in be-bop, blues, gospel and other genres. Her remarkable career included performances with such greats as Duke Ellington, Oscar Peterson and Count Basie, and she recorded no fewer than three albums with Louis Armstrong. A virtuoso scat singer, Ella Fitzgerald had a pure voice, extraordinary vocal agility and a tremendous gift for improvisation, all of which earned her the sobriquet "First Lady of Jazz."

# Moon River

**Singer** **Audrey Hepburn** **Words** **Johnny Mercer**
**Music** **Harry Mancini**

Moon River wider than a mile
I'm crossing you in style someday
Old dream maker, you heartbreaker
Wherever you're going, I'm going your way
Two drifters off to see the world

There's such a lot of world to see
We're after the same rainbows end
Waiting 'round the bend
My Huckleberry friend
Moon River and me

To the general public, Henry Mancini will always be remembered as the man who composed the famous theme to *The Pink Panther*. In 1961, he wrote "Moon River" for another Blake Edward movie, *Breakfast at Tiffany's*. In the film, Audrey Hepburn plays Holly Golightly, a country girl come to New York in search of a wealthy man to marry. Wearing a sheath dress and sunglasses, cigarette holder in hand, she stares dreamily into the window displays of the famous jeweller Tiffany's, then leads her new neighbour around by the nose. Behind the capricious and sophisticated young lady, however, hides a lost young girl who expresses her pain in the song "Moon River". Sitting on a window ledge strumming a guitar, Audrey Hepburn performs the song in a gentle, sensual voice.

# Song credits

**Willow Weep for Me**
Words and music **Ann Ronell**
© 1932 Bourne Co. /
Songwriters Guild of America

**Gone With the Wind**
Words **Herb Magidson** Music **Allie Wrubel**
© 1937 Bourne Co.

**It Might As Well Be Spring**
Words **Oscar Hammerstein II**
Music **Richard Rodgers**
© 1945 Renewed Williamson Music,
an Imagem company
Lyrics used by permission
of **Williamson Music**

**Come Rain or Come Shine**
From **St. Louis Woman** Words **Johnny Mercer**
Music **Harold Arlen** © 1946 Renewed The
Johnny Mercer Foundation and S.A. Music Co.
All rights for The **Johnny Mercer**
Foundation administered by WB Music Corp.
Lyrics used by permission of **Alfred Music**
and **Hal Leonard Corporation**

**Stormy Weather**
From **Cotton Club Parade of 1933**
Words **Ted Koehler** Music **Harold Arlen**
© 1933 Renewed (1961) Fred Ahlert Music
Group (ASCAP) / Ted Koehler Music (ASCAP)
administered by BMG Rights Management (US)
LLC and S.A. Music Co. administered by EMI
Mills Music Inc. Lyrics used by permission of
**Alfred Music** and **Hal Leonard Corporation**

**Blue Moon**
Words **Lorenz Hart** Music **Richard Rodgers**
© 1934 Renewed Metro-Goldwyn-Mayer Inc.
All rights administered by EMI Robbins
Catalog Inc. Lyrics used by permission
of **Alfred Music**

**The Snow Is Falling**
Words and Music by **Jeremy Leiber**
and **Mike Stoller** © 1953 Renewed Sony/
ATV Music Publishing LLC
All rights administered by Sony/ATV Music
Publishing LLC Lyrics used by permission
of **Hal Leonard Corporation**

**Let It Snow! Let It Snow! Let It Snow!**
Words **Sammy Cahn** Music **Jule Styne**
© 1945 Renewed Producers Music Publ. Co.
Inc. and Cahn Music Company
All Rights on behalf of **Producers Music Publ.
Co. Inc.** administered by Chappell & Co. Inc.
Lyrics used by permission of **Alfred Music**
and **Imagem**

**December**
Words and music **Al Rinker**
and **Floyd Huddleston**
© 1949 Renewed WB Music Corp
and Popoosa Music
Lyrics used permission of **Alfred Music**

**Winter Weather**
Words and music **Ted Shapiro**
© 1941 Renewed Leo Feist Inc. assigned
to EMI Catalogue Partnership All rights
administered by EMI Feist Catalogue Inc.
Lyrics used by permission of **Alfred Music**

**What Are You Doing New Year's Eve?**
Words and music **Frank Loesser**
© 1947 Frank Music Corp., a division
of MPL Music Publishing Inc. Lyrics used
by permission of **Hal Leonard Corporation**

**Moon River**
From the Paramount Picture
**Breakfast at Tiffany's**
Words **Johnny Mercer**
Music **Harry Mancini** © 1961 Renewed
Sony/ATV Music Publishing LLC
All rights administered by Sony/ATV
Music Publishing LLC Lyrics used by
permission of **Hal Leonard Corporation**

## STORYBOOK - MUSIC CD TITLES
## ALSO AVAILABLE ON THE SECRET MOUNTAIN

### Dreams Are Made for Children
Classic Jazz Lullabies
Performed by **Ella Fitzgerald, Sarah Vaughan, Billie Holiday…**
Selected by **Misja Fitzgerald Michel**
Illustrated by **Ilya Green**

### Sleep Softly
Classical Lullabies by **Brahms, Schubert, Satie, Debussy…**
Performed by **L'Ensemble Agora**
Illustrated by **Élodie Nouhen**

### Tomorrow is a Chance to Start Over
Bedtime Story and Dream Songs by **Hilary Grist**

### Dream Songs Night Songs From Mali to Louisiana
Lullabies From Around the World
Bedtime Story by **Patrick Lacoursière**
Illustrated by **Sylvie Bourbonnière**

Song selection **Misja Fitzgerald Michel** Illustrations **Ilya Green**
Explanatory notes **Françoise Tenier**
Translation **David Lytle and Hélène Roulston** (Service d'édition Guy Connolly)
Copy editing **Ruth Joseph** Editing, mixing and mastering **Dominique Ledolley**
Graphic Design **Célestin Forestier, Frédérique Renoust and Stephan Lorti**

Aknowledgements **Bibliothéque nationale de France (Audio-Visual Department)**

☉ **www.thesecretmountain.com**
ⓒ ⓟ **2016 The Secret Mountain (Folle Avoine Productions)**
**ISBN 10: 2-924217-78-4    ISBN 13: 978-2-924217-78-8**

First published in France by Didier Jeunesse, Paris, 2015